JUNIOR
GRAPHIC NOVEL

FINDING NEMO

Adapted by Charles Bazaldua

Artwork by Claudio Sciarrone
Gabriella Matta
Davide Baldoni

DISNEP
PRESS

New York

Copyright © 2006 Disney Enterprises, Inc.
Finding Nemo © 2003 Disney Enterprises, Inc./Pixar

No part of this book may be reproduced or transmitted in any form or by any means, electronic or mechanical, including photocopying, recording, or by any information storage and retrieval system, without written permission from the publisher. For information address Disney Press, 114 Fifth Avenue, New York, New York 10011-5690.

Printed in the United States of America
First U.S. Edition
1 3 5 7 9 10 8 6 4 2
ISBN 1-4231-0140-5

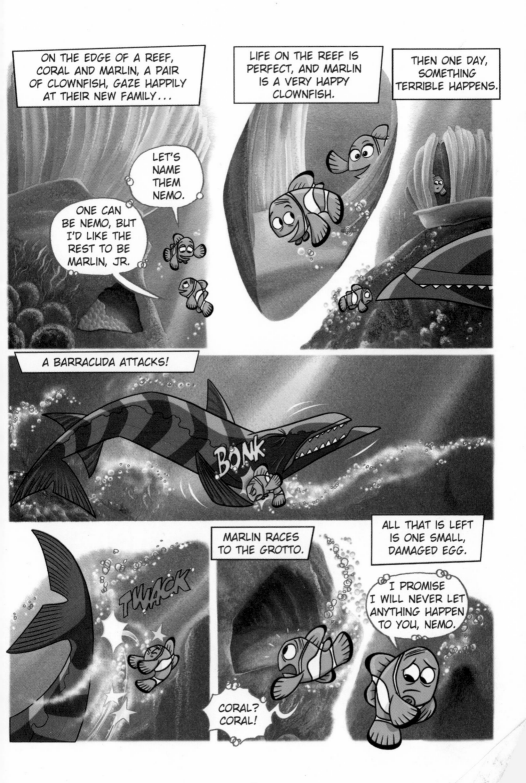

3

4

5

6

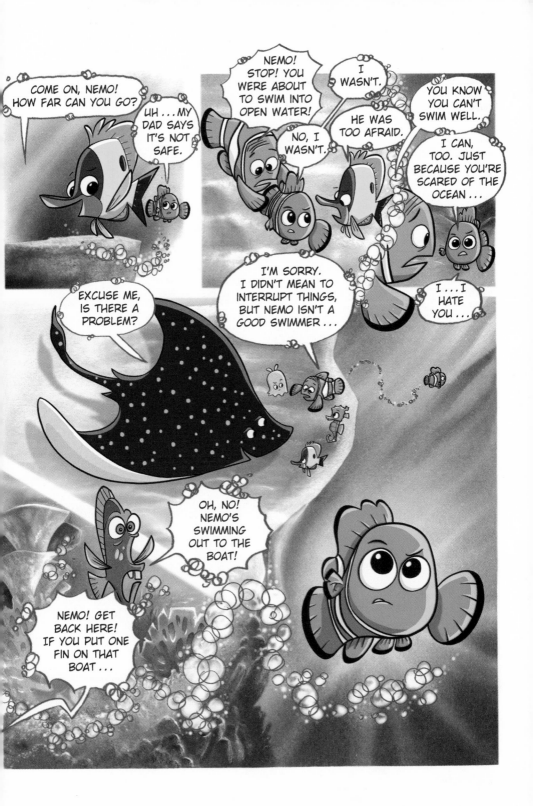

11

13

14

15

MEANWHILE, NEMO IS PLUNGED INTO A STRANGE, NEW PLACE...

...AN AQUARIUM IN A DENTIST'S OFFICE.

I FOUND THAT POOR LITTLE GUY ON THE REEF AND SAVED HIM.

GASP!

BUUUUUUUUBBLES!

AAAAH!

TAKE IT EASY, LITTLE FELLAH.

AW, DON'T BE SCARED, DEAR.

I WANNA GO HOME. DO YOU KNOW WHERE MY DAD IS?

BUT... I'M FROM THE OCEAN.

THE OCEAN!! AAAAH! HE HASN'T BEEN DECONTAMINATED YET!

MY NAME IS DEB.

VOILA! HE IS CLEAN.

YOUR DAD'S PROBABLY BACK AT THE PET STORE.

18

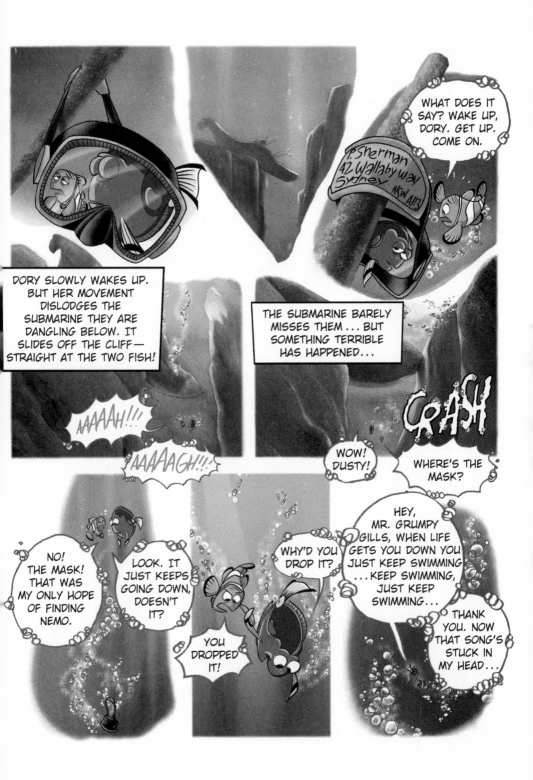

20

21

GO EASY ON HIM. HE'S LOST HIS SON, FABIO. DO YOU KNOW HOW TO GET TO SYDNEY?

FOLLOW THE EAC—THAT'S UH, THE EAST AUSTRALIAN CURRENT.

DORY, YOU DID IT! LET'S GO!

ONE MORE THING. AT THE TRENCH... SWIM THROUGH IT... NOT OVER IT!

TRENCH. THROUGH ...NOT OVER ...I'LL REMEMBER.

OW, OW, OW! HOW COME IT DIDN'T STING YOU?

IT DID. BUT I LIVE IN AN ANEMONE. I'M USED TO THESE KINDS OF STINGS. AT LEAST IT WAS JUST A LITTLE ONE.

OKAY!

LOOK! SOMETHING SHINY! IT SWAM OVER THE TRENCH. LET'S FOLLOW IT.

BAD TRENCH. WE'LL SWIM OVER.

WE SHOULD SWIM "THROUGH IT, NOT OVER IT." TRUST ME.

AAAAH!!!

DON'T MOVE! THIS IS BAD!

24

25

26

28

29

31

AAAAAHHH!!!

WOOOSH

LOOK! S-SI-SIDN- SYDNEY!

SYDNEY NEW SOUTHWALE

WE'RE GONNA FIND MY SON! ALL WE HAVE TO DO IS FIND THE BOAT THAT TOOK HIM.

THAT SHOULD BE EASY.

YOU WERE RIGHT, DORY. WE MADE IT!

BUT BACK AT THE DENTIST'S OFFICE, TIME IS RUNNING OUT.

MORNING, EVERYONE! THE SUN IS SHINING, THE TANK IS CLEAN AND ... THE TANK IS CLEAN!

THE BOSS MUST HAVE INSTALLED A NEW SYSTEM WHILE WE WERE SLEEPING.

THE AQUASCUM CLEANS YOUR TANK EVERY 5 MINUTES.

CURSE YOU, AQUASCUM.

THE ESCAPE PLAN IS RUINED.

WHAT ARE WE GONNA DO?

DARLA!

KEEP OUTTA SIGHT, KID!

33

34

37

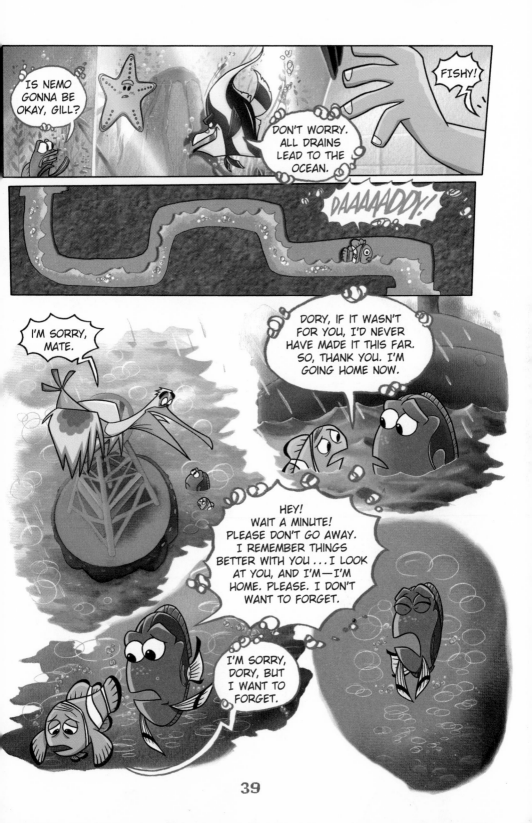

39

40

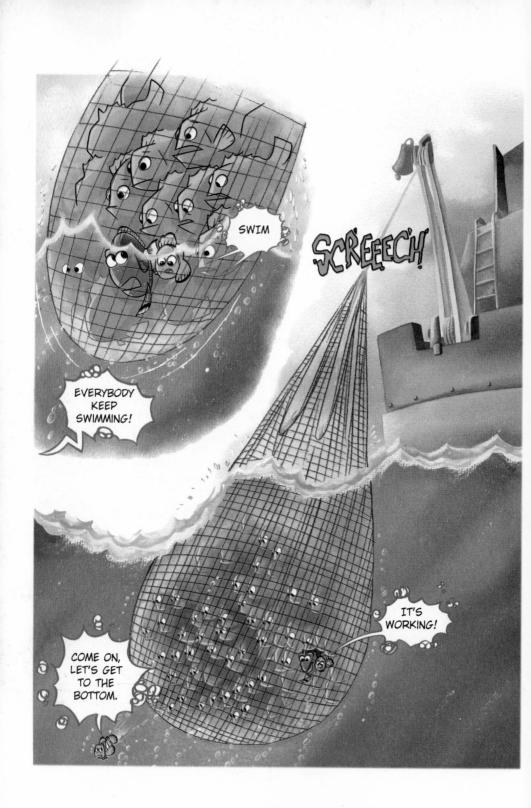

44

AND ONE FINE DAY, BACK IN SYDNEY...
THE DENTIST'S AQUARIUM FILTER BREAKS.
THE DENTIST IS LEFT TO CLEAN IT ALL
BY HIMSELF...

SPLASH

SPLASH

...AND WOULDN'T YOU KNOW,
HIS BAGGED FISH ESCAPE TO
THE HARBOR...AND FREEDOM.

THE END